Eve Shaw

Grandmother's Alphabet

Pfeifer-Hamilton
Duluth, Minnesota

Pfeifer-Hamilton Publishers
210 West Michigan
Duluth, MN 55802-1908
218-727-0500

Grandmother's Alphabet

Printed by Doosan Dong-A Co., Ltd.
10 9 8 7 6 5 4 3 2

Editorial Director: Susan Gustafson
Graphic Design: Jeff Brownell

Library of Congress Catalog Card Number: 96-60669
ISBN 1-57025-127-4
Printed in the Republic of Korea

For grandmothers everywhere,
for my own lovely grandmother, Eva Peterson,
and for my surrogate grandchildren,
Reland Ann Tuomi and John Messenger Symons.

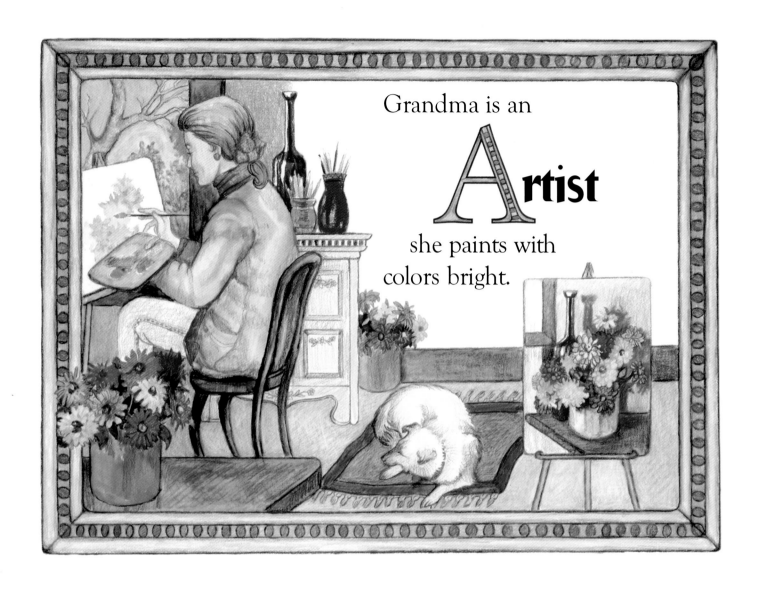

Grandma is an

Artist

she paints with
colors bright.

Grandma can be...
an actress, an author, or an architect
...and so can I.

Grandma is a

Business-woman

who often works at night.

Grandma can be…
a bookseller, a banker, or a bird-watcher
…and so can I.

Grandma is a

Carpenter

who crafts things
out of wood.

Grandma can be...
a cashier, a coach, or a computer operator
...and so can I.

Grandma is a
Doctor
she helps children to
feel good.

Grandma can be…
a designer, a dentist, or a day-care provider
…and so can I.

Grandma is an

Engineer

she plans bridges,
roads, and towers.

Grandma can be…
an entertainer, an editor, or an executive
…and so can I.

Grandma is a

Florist

creating lovely
gifts from flowers.

Grandma can be…
a firefighter, a forester, or a family counselor
…and so can I.

Grandma is a **Gardener** growing corn and daisies too.

Grandma can be...
a grocer, a guide, or a Girl Scout leader
...and so can I.

Grandma is a **H**ome-**maker**

there's nothing she
can't do.

Grandma can be…
a hair stylist, a horse trainer, or a historian
…and so can I.

Grandma is an

Innkeeper

folks stay with her
when they travel.

Grandma can be…
an inspector, an ice skater, or an interior decorator
…and so can I.

Grandma is a

Judge

dispensing justice with her gavel.

Grandma can be…
a jeweler, a juggler, or a journalist
…and so can I.

Grandma is a
Kitemaker
her kites soar like
birds on string.

Grandma can be...
a knitter, a kayaker, or a kindergarten teacher
...and so can I.

Grandma is a

Librarian

who loans
books on everything.

Grandma can be…
a lifeguard, a lawyer, or a legislator
…and so can I.

Grandma is a

Magician

she has secrets
she won't tell.

Grandma can be…
a minister, a mechanic, or a mayor
…and so can I.

Grandma is a
Nurse
who keeps
me safe and well.

Grandma can be…
a naturalist, a neighbor, or a newscaster
…and so can I.

Grandma is an

Oceanographer
she explores the
deep blue seas.

Grandma can be...
an optometrist, an organist, or an occupational therapist
...and so can I.

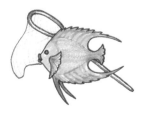

Grandma is a **P**ilot flying high above the trees.

Grandma can be…
a plumber, a police officer, or a printer
…and so can I.

Grandma is a
Quilter
whose patterns
shine and glitter.

Grandma can be...
a quartet member or a quality controller
...and so can I.

Grandma is a

Rancher

she can tend
to any critter.

Grandma can be…
a receptionist, a realtor, or a reporter,
…and so can I.

Grandma is a **S**cientist she knows what's inside a seed.

Grandma can be...
a senator, a student, or a secretary
...and so can I.

Grandma is a **T**eacher helping children learn to read.

Grandma can be…
a therapist, a travel agent, or a television star
…and so can I.

Grandma makes **Umbrellas** to keep me dry in rain or sleet.

Grandma can be...
an umpire, an upholsterer, or a university president
...and so can I.

Grandma is a
Violinist
she plays music
soft and sweet.

Grandma can be...
a volunteer, a vintner, or a vocational counselor
...and so can I.

Grandma is a **W**eaver designing rugs in soft warm tones.

Grandma can be…
a waitress, a welder, or a wedding consultant
…and so can I.

Grandma is an

X-ray technician

she takes pictures
of your bones.

Grandma can be…
a xylophonist
…and so can I.

Grandma is a
Yachter
she sails her boat
on the summer breeze.

Grandma can be...
a yarn spinner, a youth worker, or a yoga instructor
...and so can I.

Grandma is a

Zoologist

who studies
chimpanzees.

Grandma can be…
a zookeeper or a zillion other things
…and so can I.

There are so many
grandmas with lives from

A to Z

but grandmas have in common
grandchildren just like me.

Now let's see what I can be!

administrative assistant
air traffic controller
ambulance driver
announcer
anthropologist
antique dealer
archeologist
astronaut
athelete
auto worker
baker
beekeeper
biologist
board member
bookkeeper
caretaker
cartoonist
caterer
chemist
chiropractor
choir director
conservationist
consultant
cook
court reporter
cyclist
dancer
dental hygienist
dietitian

drama critic
EKG technician
electrician
entrepreneur
factory worker
farmer
fashion designer
film producer
flight attendant
fund-raiser
geographer
graphic designer
home health aide
hotel manager
housekeeper
insurance agent
janitor
job trainer
lab technician
mail carrier
manager
meteorologist
mortician
naval officer
nursing assistant
obstetrician
painter
paramedic
peace worker
personnel manager
pianist
physical therapist
playground supervisor
principal

proof reader
psychologist
rabbi
radio announcer
researcher
restaurant manager
sales representative
seamstress
security guard
singer
sign painter
sociologist
sportscaster
storyteller
surveyor
tax consultant
taxi driver
teller
textile worker
tutor
union organizer
urban planner
vicar
weathercaster

A B C D

H I J

N O P

U V W